W9-CAD-617

A NOTE TO PARENTS

When your children are ready to "step into reading," giving them the right books—and lots of them—is as crucial as giving them the right food to eat. **Step into Reading Books** present exciting stories and information reinforced with lively, colorful illustrations that make learning to read fun, satisfying, and worthwhile. They are priced so that acquiring an entire library of them is affordable. And they are beginning readers with an important difference—they're written on four levels.

Step 1 Books, with their very large type and extremely simple vocabulary, have been created for the very youngest readers. **Step 2 Books** are both longer and slightly more difficult. **Step 3 Books,** written to mid-second-grade reading levels, are for the child who has acquired even greater reading skills. **Step 4 Books** offer exciting nonfiction for the increasingly proficient reader.

Children develop at different ages. **Step into Reading Books,** with their four levels of reading, are designed to help children become good—and interested—readers *faster*. The grade levels assigned to the four steps—preschool through grade 1 for Step 1, grades 1 through 3 for Step 2, grades 2 and 3 for Step 3, and grades 2 through 4 for Step 4—are intended only as guides. Some children move through all four steps very rapidly; others climb the steps over a period of several years. These books will help your child "step into reading" in style!

For Jane
—J. O'C.

To my children, Scott, Megan,
Jamie, Chris, and Brandon
—J. C.

Photo credits: AP/Wide World Photos, pp. 34, 47, 48; Focus on Sports, cover (upper left, upper right, and lower right), pp. 17, 23, 25; Marvin E. Newman/*Sports Illustrated*, p. 12; John Pierce/ Allsport, p. 38; Ken Regan/Camera 5, pp. 35, 36; UPI/Bettmann Newsphotos, cover (lower left), pp. 11, 13, 14, 15; Gerard Vandystadt/*Sports Illustrated,* p. 42.

Text copyright © 1992 by Jim O'Connor
Illustrations copyright © 1992 by Jim Campbell
Library of Congress Cataloging-in-Publication Data
O'Connor, Jim.
    Comeback! : four true stories / by Jim O'Connor ; illustrated by Jim Campbell.
        p.   cm. – (Step into reading. A Step 4 book)
    Summary: Describes how four famous athletes overcame serious injuries or debilitating conditions to become superstars.
    ISBN 0-679-82666-1 (trade) – ISBN 0-679-92666-6 (lib. bdg.)   1. Athletes–United States–Biography–Juvenile literature.   2. Athletes–Wounds and injuries–United States–Juvenile literature.   [1. Athletes–Wounds and injuries.]   I. Campbell, Jim, 1942-   .   II. Title. III. Series: Step into reading. Step 4 book. GV697.A1026 1992   796'.092'2–dc20 [B]   91-25028

Manufactured in the United States of America   10 9 8 7 6

STEP INTO READING is a trademark of Random House, Inc.

Step into Reading

Comeback!
Four True Stories

By Jim O'Connor
Illustrated by Jim Campbell

A Step into Sports Step 4 Book

Random House 🏠 New York

Wilma Rudolph

It is a hot summer day in 1960. Rome's Olympic Stadium is packed. Down on the track, eight young women take their places for the 100-meter dash.

This is the fastest Olympic event. It lasts only a few seconds. But in those seconds the runner must use every bit of strength, skill, and stamina to win.

When the race is over, a tall, thin black woman from the United States has won. She is awarded the first of the three gold medals she will take home. Her name is Wilma Rudolph. By the time the Olympics end, she is called the "Fastest Woman in the World."

Wilma made it all look easy. Few people could have guessed the incredible obstacles this star athlete had faced. Poverty. Prejudice. And a deadly disease that crippled her for most of her childhood.

Wilma was born in Tennessee in 1940. She grew up in a small town called Clarksville. Her parents already had 16 other children. They were very poor.

Wilma was a tiny, sickly baby, but she hung on. Then at four Wilma came down with a terrible illness called polio.

From the 1930s through the early 1950s, polio killed thousands of children and left many more in wheelchairs. The "lucky" ones could only walk with their legs in iron braces.

Polio crippled Wilma's left leg. Doctors said she would walk with a brace for the rest of her life. But Wilma's mother refused to believe them. She took Wilma to a hospital where specialists worked to make Wilma's leg stronger.

In the 1950s, blacks could not eat in the

same restaurants or go to the same schools or hospitals as whites. Wilma and her mother had to travel 50 miles each way for Wilma's treatments. They did it for years.

The treatments were painful. Wilma's leg was stretched and rubbed. And every night Wilma's mother or one of her brothers or sisters stretched and rubbed the leg some more.

When Wilma started first grade, she still wore the brace. She hated it. The

brace was heavy and ugly. Its leather straps hurt.

Wilma felt bad. While her friends ran and jumped and played games, she could only sit and watch. Some kids made fun of her.

Wilma's family would cheer her up and encourage her. Slowly her leg started to get stronger. She began taking off the brace when she was at home. By the time she was ten, Wilma only had to wear it to school. And on one unforgettable day two years later, she took off the brace and never used it again.

Now at last Wilma could get off the sidelines and into the action. She decided to play basketball. Wilma was a natural on the court. In high school she scored 32 points in her first varsity game!

And the team made it to the state conference championships with Wilma as its star. They didn't win, but that tournament was very important for Wilma.

A track coach for Tennessee State University, Ed Temple, saw Wilma play. Right away he knew her long legs and skinny build were perfect for a sprinter—someone who can run short distances very fast.

He invited Wilma to spend the summer at Tennessee State with other high school girls learning about track. In a few short weeks, she learned the secrets of sprinting: how to time her start, how to breathe properly, how to move her arms and legs correctly. She trained hard and got stronger and faster.

Her summer in Nashville paid off. Wilma ran against the nation's best young runners at the Amateur Athletic Union (AAU) championships in Philadelphia. And she won two events!

Best of all, she got to meet Jackie Robinson. Jackie was the first black man to play major-league baseball and a true superstar. Jackie told her something she never forgot: "Don't let anything or anybody keep you from running."

Then Wilma qualified for the 1956 Olympic Games in Melbourne, Australia!

At 16 she was the youngest member of the team. Wilma felt bad about beating older runners and maybe hurting their feelings. But another runner, Mae Faggs, helped Wilma develop a winning attitude. Mae made her see that it was all right to win no matter who she beat. That was what being the best meant.

At the '56 Olympics, Wilma saw athletes of all colors and cultures compete. And the women's 400-meter relay team, with Wilma running third, staged an upset and took the bronze medal for third place.

When Wilma returned to Clarksville with her Olympic medal, she was surprised to find that she was a hometown star! People, even white people, stopped her on the street and shook her hand. There was a ceremony in her honor.

After high school Wilma went to Tennessee State University on a full scholarship. College was tough for Wilma, but she made a "B" average and became the fastest sprinter on the Tennessee State Tigerbelles squad.

By the 1960 Olympics, Wilma was the best woman sprinter in America. She easily qualified for the 100- and 200-meter dashes. And she and three other Tiger-belles qualified for the 400-meter relay.

When the U.S. team got to Rome, the

temperature was almost 100° F. But the heat didn't bother the Tigerbelles—the weather was the same back home.

Just before the games began, Wilma twisted her ankle. But that didn't stop her. She breezed into the 100-meter finals. She won her first gold medal by running the 100 meters in a blazing 11.0 seconds. In the 200 meters, she took another gold.

Wilma's final event was the 400-meter relay. The relay is a tricky race. Each of the first three runners must sprint 100 meters before handing a short stick, called a baton, to the next runner. The last runner, or "anchor," finishes the race. If the baton is dropped, the entire team is disqualified.

Wilma was the anchor. She nearly lost the baton when it was passed to her. Then she overtook the Russian and German runners to win! "The feeling of

accomplishment welled up inside of me," Wilma later recalled. "Three Olympic gold medals. I knew that was something no one could ever take away."

Wilma became world famous. In France they called her "La Perle Noire"

(The Black Pearl). Italy named her "La Gazzèlla Nera" (The Black Gazelle).

When Wilma returned to the United States, she met President John F. Kennedy and toured the country.

Clarksville had a homecoming parade for her. And there was a big dinner in her honor. It was the first time in the history of Clarksville that blacks and whites ate together.

Wilma graduated from Tennessee State in 1963. Over the next years she married, taught elementary school, coached track, and raised a family. Today she is one of the best known and most respected women ever to run track in the United States.

Catfish Hunter

On a hot Sunday in 1987, thousands of baseball fans crowded the streets of Cooperstown, New York. They were there to see the newest members of the Baseball Hall of Fame.

An extra-large group had come all the way from the little farming town of Hertford, North Carolina, to honor its most famous hometown boy, Jim "Catfish" Hunter.

Practically every fan in Cooperstown knew that Catfish Hunter had pitched on five World Series championship teams. He had won 224 games in his career. He was a superstar on the two superstar teams of the 1970s—the Oakland A's and the New York Yankees. If anyone deserved to be in

the Hall of Fame, it was Catfish. But there was an amazing story behind his rise to baseball stardom.

Born on a farm in Hertford in 1946, Jimmy Hunter was the youngest of ten children. He and his brothers played lots of baseball, even though the family couldn't always afford a real ball. Sometimes the boys played with potatoes or even corncobs. "Anything that was round and firm," Catfish remembered.

Jimmy learned a lot from those back-yard games. He had to throw strikes or his big brothers wouldn't let him play.

By the time he was twelve, everyone

knew that Jim Hunter could throw heat. He could strike out anyone—even boys who were much older. And like lots of kids, he dreamed of a baseball career.

As early as his junior year in high school, it looked as if his dream would come true. Pro scouts came to watch him play. They were already talking about big-league contracts.

Then came Thanksgiving, 1964. That day Jim and his brothers Pete and Ray went hunting, as they often did. Halfway home Pete's gun suddenly went off and knocked Jim over. He looked down and saw blood pouring from his foot.

Jim passed out and woke up in the hospital to heartbreaking news. There were 45 shotgun pellets in his right foot. And the blast had blown off his little toe.

Jim's father was sitting next to the bed. "Looks like my baseball career is over, Daddy," Jim said.

Jim knew that a pitcher needs more than a good arm to pitch. He uses his feet and legs too. A right-hander like Jim balances on his right leg for a second while his left leg kicks up and forward. As he comes around to deliver the ball, he pushes off with his right foot. This gives him the power he needs. A foot injury can end a pitcher's career. It looked as if Jim's would never begin.

Jim was on crutches for weeks. Afterward he still had a bad limp. And every step hurt.

Most baseball scouts lost interest in Jim. But not Clyde Kluttz, a scout for the Kansas City A's. Clyde played catch with Jim to cheer him up. He gave Jim tips on speeding up his recovery. Clyde saw something that the rest of the scouts missed. Jim Hunter wouldn't give up.

In his senior year, Jim was back on the mound. His foot still hurt when he pitched, so he put pieces of foam rubber in his shoe to ease the pain. The baseball team opened with eight straight shutouts. Jim had two no-hitters.

Suddenly the scouts were interested again. But thanks to Clyde Kluttz, Jim signed with the Kansas City A's.

At that time Charlie Finley was the owner of the A's. Finley was always thinking up crazy gimmicks to get people to games. (Once he let any man who was bald into the park free.) And he thought fans liked players with nicknames.

Jim didn't have a nickname.

Finley told him, "When you were six years old, you ran away from home and went fishing. When they finally found you …you'd caught two big fish…catfish. And that's how you got your nickname. Okay?"

"Yes sir, Mr. Finley," "Catfish" Hunter replied.

Charlie Finley sent Catfish to the best doctors. By the start of the 1965 season, his foot didn't bother him anymore. Catfish went straight to the majors.

When Catfish joined the A's, they were

not only a losing team. They were in last place. For the next three seasons, Catfish and the A's struggled together. Catfish had a below-average record—30 wins and 36 losses.

Then, on May 8, 1968, he pitched a "perfect game." No runs were scored. And not one man reached first base. It was the first perfect game by an American League pitcher in 46 years. Suddenly Catfish was very famous.

In 1971, he had the first of five straight seasons in which he won 20 or more games. By 1974, Catfish was a proven champion and the A's had won three straight World Series. But then Catfish and Charlie Finley had a big argument about Catfish's salary.

Catfish's old friend Clyde Kluttz was now a scout for the New York Yankees. Catfish signed with them for what was then the biggest paycheck in baseball history.

Catfish's first year with the Yankees was just what the Yankees had hoped for. He finished with a 23–14 record and a 2.58 ERA. Catfish pitched more innings in more games than any Yankee pitcher in over ten years. But all those innings and all those pitches hurt Catfish. Whenever he threw the ball, he would feel a stab of pain in his shoulder.

Catfish managed to notch his 200th career victory in 1976. But when his contract with the Yankees expired in 1979, Catfish retired. He wanted to go back to Hertford and be a farmer, just like his dad.

Catfish had been a major-league ballplayer for 15 years. He was the youngest starter in baseball at age 19 and pitched a perfect game when he was just 22. He won the Cy Young Award—for the league's best pitcher—at age 28. Jim "Catfish" Hunter had come back from disaster and earned his spot in the Baseball Hall of Fame.

Bart Conner

To the millions of people who watched the 1984 Olympics in Los Angeles, Bart Conner had everything a gymnast needs to get the gold. Skill. Power. Control. Grace.

But it was amazing that Bart was even at the Olympics. Only eight months earlier he'd suffered a terrible injury. His career seemed to be over.

Bart's gymnastic talent showed early. As a kid, he did backflips off moving swings. He jumped from roofs into bushes. In fourth grade he took his first real gymnastics lessons. He was so good the gym teacher had Bart train with the high school team!

Bart learned that men's gymnastics was more than doing backflips. A gym-

nast has to master six different events, from performing tricks while hanging from two rings to doing a kind of tumbling act called the floor exercise. Bart was great at the floor exercise. He was also outstanding on the parallel bars.

When he was 11, Bart started entering meets. Before long he was winning them. Bart loved the competition. Soon he had one big goal—an Olympic gold medal. He got his chance when he made the Olympic team in 1976. He was only 18 and did not do well. But he promised himself he would win at the 1980 Olympics in Moscow.

Over the next four years, Bart became one of the best gymnasts in the United States. He easily qualified for the 1980 Olympic team. Bart was ready for Moscow —and a medal.

But in 1979, the Soviet Union invaded the country of Afghanistan. As a protest, the United States refused to let any Americans take part in the Moscow games. It would be four years until the next Olympics. Would Bart still be in top form? He was determined to hold on.

Then Bart suffered a serious injury. He ripped his right biceps muscle, a very important muscle for a gymnast. It is the main muscle of the upper arm—the one that "pops up" when a person bends his arm back toward his shoulder. A gymnast needs strong biceps to go from move to move during his routines.

It took a year and a half for Bart to recover completely.

Then in December of 1983, Bart went to Japan to compete in an important meet. On the first day, Bart was performing on the rings. All of a sudden he heard a loud ripping sound. His left biceps had snapped off his arm bone. Bart had never quit in the middle of a routine. But he stopped then and there. He knew at once that the

meet, and perhaps his career, was over.

As he left the floor, one of the Soviet coaches stopped him. "No more gymnastics for you," the coach said. "Goodbye, L.A." Bart knew it was a mean thing to say, but probably right. The Olympics were only eight months away. And 1984 was his last chance. Bart couldn't wait another four years.

Back home in America, doctors examined Bart. He got more bad news. Besides the torn muscle, there were many bone chips "floating" in Bart's elbow.

Bart needed a four-hour operation.

For the first hour the doctor worked to reattach the muscle to the upper arm bone. First he had to drill a hole into the bone. Then the tendon—the fibers that hold the muscle to the bone—was knotted and the knot "pushed" into the hole.

After that the doctor carefully cleaned the bone chips out of Bart's elbow.

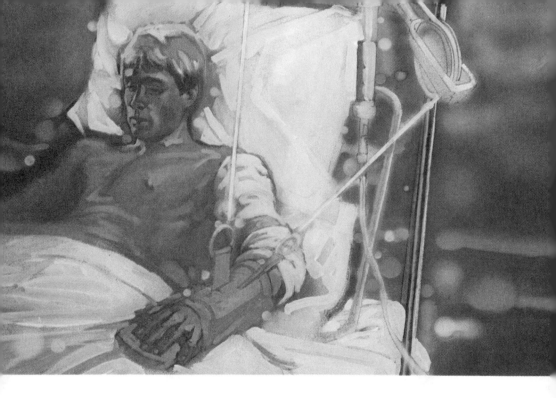

For the next two days a machine moved Bart's arm back and forth all the time to keep the muscles from stiffening up. Then the really hard part started. The doctors called it physical therapy. Bart called it torture.

Bart had to do painful exercises. And during every workout his arm and shoulder were packed in crushed ice for up to 90 minutes. Even though the rest of his body was wrapped in blankets, Bart's teeth still chattered from the cold.

Weeks later Bart began training again. He found that even the easy moves seemed hard. Still he kept trying. There was no time to spare.

In April, Bart entered his first competition since his injury. He fell off the parallel bars, and his scores in the other events were barely average. Three weeks later he did just as badly at the National Championships.

Now Bart could make the Olympics only if he scored high—very high—at the Olympic trials. For the next three weeks it was practice, practice, practice—and more practice.

Bart placed sixth—just high enough to make the Olympic team!

The Los Angeles Olympics opened July 28. Bart and his teammates faced some of the toughest competition ever.

In the team competition the United States scored an incredible upset when they beat the Chinese team to win the gold medal. Bart's high scores played a key part.

Now he had a chance to win a gold medal on his own in the floor exercise. But he was still so excited about the team competition that he couldn't concentrate. He finished in fifth place.

The U.S. coach told Bart to get serious. He had qualified in only one more event—the parallel bars. This was his last chance for the gold.

The competition was intense. Going into the final round, Bart had a lead of only 25 thousandths of a point over a Japanese gymnast. When the Japanese scored a perfect 10, the pressure was really on. To win, Bart had to finish with a perfect score.

He did it! From his "free hip hand-stand" mount to his "double backflip" dismount, Bart "nailed" every move.

When the scoreboard showed 10's from every judge, Bart saw his Olympic dream come true. Only eight months after major surgery he had grabbed the gold.

Greg LeMond

The Tour de France is the most important bicycle race in the world. It travels about 2,500 miles around Europe over quiet country roads, twisting mountain passes, and busy city streets.

The 1989 Tour de France

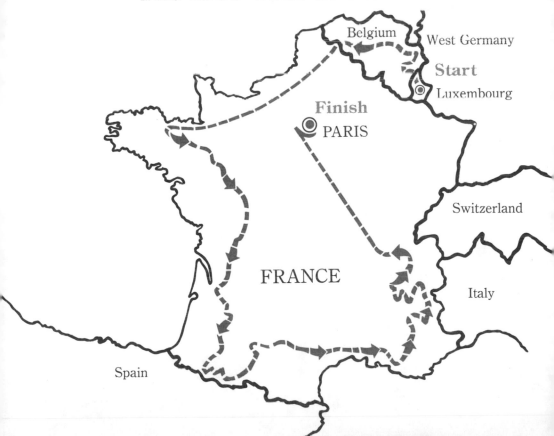

In Europe, bicycle racing is bigger than the Super Bowl is here. Bigger even than the World Series. And for three weeks each summer the race swings through France like a traveling circus and rock concert rolled into one. When the Tour ends in Paris, the winner is the world's number one cyclist.

In 1986, for the first time ever, an American won the Tour. He was a 24-year-old from Utah named Greg LeMond. Overnight Greg became internationally famous. And his future as a top racer seemed guaranteed. But only a few

months later everything changed. Greg nearly died, shot in the back in a freak hunting accident. No one knew if he would ever walk again, let alone race.

Greg had always loved sports that he could do on his own—hunting, backpacking, and freestyle skiing. When he was 14, he went to a camp for skiers. One of the best ways to stay in shape, he was told, was bicycle riding. And that's how it started. Greg and his dad, who was trying to lose a little weight, rode 20 miles every day.

Soon Greg entered races for 14- and 15-year-olds and won almost every one. He became almost unbeatable in the United States. But being number one in the U.S. didn't count for much. All the top cyclists raced in Europe. Could Greg beat *them*? When he was 16, Greg decided to find out. He entered the World Championship for Juniors—and finished ninth.

That race showed Greg that he needed to compete regularly in Europe. He began racing in Switzerland, France, and Belgium. Then, in 1980, Greg took a big step. He joined one of the world's best professional bicycle racing teams, Renault. That meant he would be paid while he trained and raced.

At first Greg had a tough time with his teammates. He didn't speak their language or understand the way they trained. Greg liked to sleep with the windows open. The French thought that fresh air was bad for a racer. They liked to eat big, two-hour-long meals. Greg was a "junk-food junkie" who liked a quick hamburger.

Sometimes Greg was tempted to quit and return home. But if he wanted to be a world-class racer, he had to stay in Europe. Greg raced almost non-stop during the next three years. And in 1983, he surprised everyone by winning the World Championships.

Now Greg felt ready for the big one—the 1984 Tour de France. His Renault teammate, Laurent Fignon, was favored to win. Greg thought he had a chance too. But Fignon was unbeatable. Still, Greg's third-place finish was tremendous for someone in his first Tour.

Then Greg switched to the La Vie Claire team. Its number one rider was Bernard Hinault—a four-time Tour de France winner and one of Greg's heroes.

Hinault told Greg he wanted to win the Tour one more time. If Greg helped him in '85, Hinault promised to help Greg win in '86. That meant Greg wouldn't try to win himself. He'd keep riders from passing Hinault. He'd even ride in front of Hinault to block the wind.

With Greg's help, Hinault won his fifth Tour in '85. But on the first 23 days of the

'86 Tour, it looked as if Hinault was going all out for another win. Finally, on the 24th day, Greg took the lead for good and won his first Tour de France.

Although Greg was thrilled with his win, he was also mad. Very mad. Greg felt that Hinault had not kept his word. Their friendship was over.

The next winter Greg went to California to visit his family. On April 20, Greg went wild-turkey hunting with his uncle and his brother-in-law. The three men separated and moved through a field of berry bushes. Greg lost sight of the others. He stopped and then began to move again. Suddenly he was hit in the back with a full blast of buckshot. His brother-in-law had accidentally shot him.

Greg's uncle ran home and called 911. Then Greg had a stroke of luck. A rescue helicopter was flying nearby. It heard the police radio calls and flew Greg to a hospital with a center for gunshot wounds.

This quick trip probably saved Greg's life. He had 60 holes in his back from the one blast of buckshot and was bleeding from every one of them. If the trip had been any longer, he would have bled to death.

Greg spent the next six days in the

hospital in terrible pain. Doctors removed most of the pellets. But two were in the lining of his heart. The doctors had to leave them there. Greg didn't know if he would ever race again.

"For three or four weeks," Greg recalled, "I'd sit at home in a chair, shaking with pain. I'd just cry and cry."

But little by little, Greg forced himself to take short walks. It was two weeks before he could go two blocks without tiring. Finally one day he climbed on his wife's bike and pedaled up and down the driveway. It wasn't the Tour de France— but Greg was riding again.

Soon Greg tried to bike a couple of miles each day. Then he took longer rides in the hills. But just as he was getting back to normal, Greg had more bad luck. He was rushed to the hospital with appendicitis. The doctors operated on him again.

That wiped out the 1987 season for Greg. He was sure he could come back to top form in 1988. But for the first time, Greg's willpower was not enough. By the '89 season, his ranking had dropped from #2 to #345!

People were saying that Greg LeMond was washed up. But he decided to race in the '89 Tour de France just the same.

In 1989, the Tour would be harder than ever. It would cover 2,025 miles in 22 days of racing. An extra day of mountain racing had been added, and there were three time trials—when the riders raced against the clock and not one another.

Laurent Fignon was a favorite. No one was betting on Greg—even he didn't expect much. His personal goal was to finish in the top 20.

He surprised himself by winning the first time trial. He began to think he had a chance after all. But Fignon kept pulling ahead. By the final day he had built up a 50-second lead.

The Tour finished with a time trial ending in Paris. Greg had only 15 miles in which to wipe out Fignon's lead. It would take a tremendous effort to win.

Greg decided to try a new kind of handlebars for this last leg. They extended out in front of his regular handlebars so

that he could ride in a stretched-out, flat position that helped him go faster.

It worked! When Greg crossed the finish line he had shut out Fignon.

Greg won his second Tour de France by the slimmest margin in Tour history—only eight seconds! But he had won. After two years of pain and defeat he had come back to his place as the world's top racer. And in 1990, he won the Tour again!